Requests for permission to make copies of any part of the work
should be mailed to the following address: Permissions Department,
Harcourt, Inc., 6277 Sea Harbor Drive, Orlando, Florida 32887-6777.

www.HarcourtBooks.com

Gulliver Books is a trademark of Harcourt, Inc., registered in
the United States of America and/or other jurisdictions.

Library of Congress Cataloging-in-Publication Data
O'Malley, Kevin, 1961–
Little buggy/by Kevin O'Malley.
p.   cm.
"Gulliver Books."
Summary: A young ladybug is determined to learn how to fly and,
with the help of his father, he succeeds.
[1. Ladybugs—Fiction.   2. Fathers and sons—Fiction.]
I. Title.   II. Series.
PZ7.O526Li   2002
[E]—dc21   2001005656
ISBN 0-15-216339-5

First edition
A C E G H F D B
Printed in Singapore

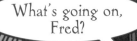

Oh, you're already up there. My, you sure are in a hurry. Okay now, take a deep breath, stretch out your wings…